2

First published in Great Britain 2004
by Egmont Books Limited
239 Kensington High Street, London W8 6SA
Story adapted from *Best Dressed Engine*
Photographs © Gullane (Thomas) Limited 2004
All Rights Reserved
ISBN 1 4052 1027 3

Thomas the Tank Engine & Friends

A BRITT ALLCROFT COMPANY PRODUCTION

Based on The Railway Series by The Rev W Awdry

© Gullane (Thomas) LLC 2004

1 3 5 7 9 10 8 6 4 2
Printed in China

Gordon and
the Competition

**Based on *The Railway Series*
by The Rev. W. Awdry**

The engines on the Island of Sodor were very excited. There was going to be a May Day celebration with music, dancing and lots of fun.

Knapford station was being decorated and The Fat Controller said the engines could be decorated, too!
"I'm going to wear blue bunting," said Murdoch.
"I'm going to wear a big red banner," said Thomas.

"I won't wear any decorations!" said Gordon. "Decorations are far too undignified for an important engine like me!"

"In that case, we'll have all the fun without you," James said.

Thomas was bringing the maypole to the village. As he went over the level crossing, a farmer and his children waved at him.

"Toot! Toot!" said Thomas in reply.

The next morning, Percy's Driver wrapped streamers and flags around his funnel. Thomas' Driver attached a red banner to Thomas. Both engines were very happy to be decorated. They could hardly wait for the May Day celebrations.

"We could have a prize for the Best Dressed Engine," said James. "It could be a competition."

"What's this? I'm sure to win any competition!" said Gordon.

"You would have to be decorated," said James.

"Not me!" said Gordon. "You'd never catch me looking so ridiculous!"

When May Day arrived, it was a beautiful sunny day. All the engines looked splendid, except Gordon. He still refused to wear any decorations at all.

Gordon told himself he was glad he wasn't taking part in the silly competition. He was much too important for that. He set off and tried to forget all about it. But secretly, Gordon felt a little left out. He wished he had joined in the fun, after all.

A colourful banner had been strung across the river bridge. It was flapping furiously in the wind. As Gordon steamed over the bridge, one end of the banner came loose. It wrapped around Gordon's firebox and flapped against his funnel. Poor Gordon couldn't see anything!

As Gordon chugged past a station, all the people laughed at him. Gordon tried to whoosh the banner off, but it wouldn't budge.

"I can't see!" Gordon whistled to his Driver. "Stop!"

"You can't stop, Gordon," said his Driver. "You're the Express!"

Gordon tried to go faster to shake off the banner, but it was stuck fast.

When Gordon arrived at Knapford, the bright banner was still flapping around his funnel.

"We didn't think you wanted to be decorated," said Thomas in surprise.

"I didn't!" said Gordon.

"Your banner is very nice, Gordon," said Percy.

"I think Gordon has won the prize,"
said James. "He's definitely the Best
Dressed Engine!"
All the engines cheered and whistled.
And Gordon was secretly pleased –
he had won the competition after all!